For L.H. and S.H.,

your hands will *always* have a place in mine.

This book is given with love

_____

From Great Gandparents

Richard @ Dorothy Gann Y-2022

Written by Heather Lean

Illustrated by Marina Reshetnikova

Edited by Karen Austin, Sheri Wall & Brooke Vitale

For all inquiries, please contact us at:

info@puppysmiles.org

To see more of our books, visit us at:

www.PuppyDogsAndIceCream.com

Wonderful Moments Ahead

Little Hands

Written by : Heather Lean Illustrated by : Marina Reshetnikova

Little hands, little hands,
holding mine so tight,
I look upon your face
and feel love at first sight.

As I gaze into your eyes,
I then *begin* to see,
All the things your little hands
will one day come to be.

*L*ittle hands, little hands,
you'll *throw* your food around,
Into your hair, on your chair,
and even on the ground.

Little hands, little hands,
crawling right along,
Your little hands and little legs
will soon become so strong.

Little hands, little hands,
will *peek* under the door,
Because you'll be so curious
and wanting to explore.

Little hands, little hands,
can surely *make* a mess,

What you'll do from day to day,
I'll never really guess.

Little hands, little hands,
will *hide* your face from view,
Then open up and close again
as we play peek-a-boo.

Little hands, little hands,
reaching out for me,
When taking your first baby steps
so excitedly.

Little hands, little hands,
will *splash* in bubbles too,
With giggles bringing so much joy
to everything we do.

*L*ittle hands, little hands, you'll be *swinging* from my arm,

Knowing I'll protect you and keep you safe from harm.

Little hands, little hands,
playing with your toys,
Happy beating drums all day,
making music with such joy!

*L*ittle hands, little hands,
you'll *share* with all your heart,
Love and hugs for your best friend,
right from the very start.

*L*ittle hands, little hands,
will *help* your mommy bake,

Sprinkling so much goodness
into all the treats we'll make.

*L*ittle hands, little hands,
will *build* upon the beach,
Like grains of sand before you,
the world's within your reach.

Little Hands, little hands,
will gently *rest* in place,
As tender kisses find their way,
toward my happy face.

*L*ittle hands, little hands,
will *ride* a brand new bike,
How quickly you will soon outgrow
your little three-wheel trike.

Little hands, little hands,
sharing what you see,

Fingers will help turn each page
when you read to me.

Little hands, little hands,
resting peacefully,

I'll wonder what's in store for you,
and what your dreams might be.

Little Hands, little hands,
will *learn* to write with pens,
Tracing over letters
and writing words again.

Little hands, little hands,
your arms will *reach* up high,

And pick a crispy apple
hanging way up in the sky.

*L*ittle hands, little hands,
will have *fun* in the tree,

To climb and view from way up high,
feeling brave and free.

*L*ittle hands, little hands,
chilling in the snow,

Making snowmen with good friends,
how quickly you will grow.

*L*ittle hands, little hands,
when *reaching* for the keys,
You'll promise me to do your best,
and put my mind at ease.

Little hands, little hands,
rocking out with friends,
Could occupy a lot of time,
even on weekends.

Little hands, little hands,
you'll *toss* that cap with joy,

And I will see my Little Hands,
now a happy grown-up boy.

Little hands, little hands,
when your first baby's *born*,
I'll cherish those new little hands
like they were my own.

$\mathcal{T}$he past, present, and future,
completely *intertwine*,
Right here in this moment
as I hold your hand in mine.

However you may *grow*
and wherever you may be,
Know that you will always
be *Little Hands* to me.

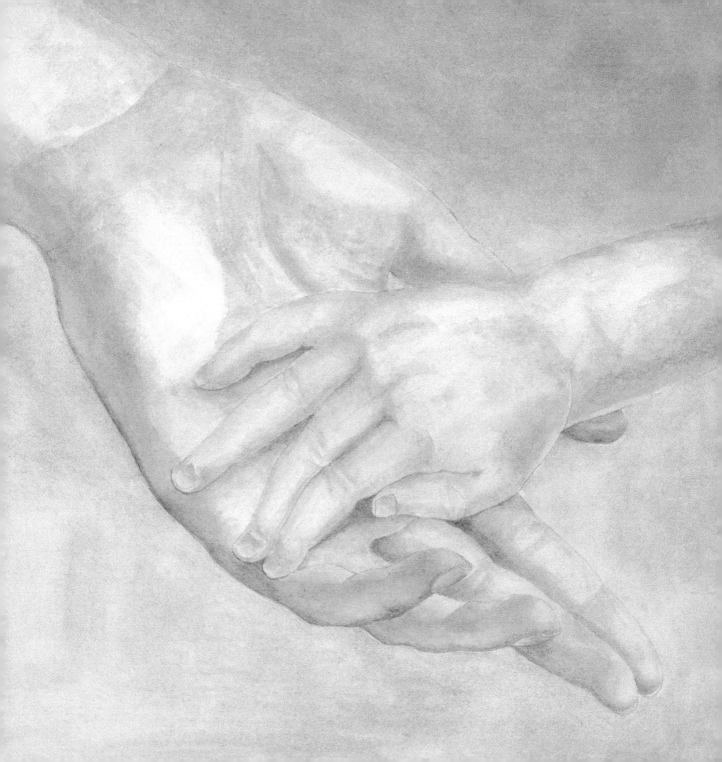

Capture the Moment

Place your child's handprint in the frame below

Name: Age: Date:

About the Author

Heather Lean is a mother of two. The inspiration for Little Hands came while watching her youngest child grow up. She always tries to remind herself to stay present in the moment and enjoy all of life's precious little treasures. Heather resides in New York, where she enjoys spending time with her family, friends, and pets. She has four hens, three cats, and a puppy named Beau.

About the Artist

Marina Reshetnikova was born in Kherson, Ukraine. She worked as a designer of agricultural machinery, but devoted much of her spare time to painting and soon this hobby became her main profession. Marina illustrated and published her first book of fairy tales in 2011. Since then, she's illustrated many more children's books. All her pictures are painted full of details and emotions, as they come to life across the pages.

Claim your FREE Gift!

 Visit:

PDICBooks.com/Gift

Thank you for purchasing

Little Hands

and welcome to the Puppy Dogs & Ice Cream family.
We're certain you're going to love the little gift
we've prepared for you at the website above.